A BANANA BOOK

THE BEAST IN THE BASEMENT

Ann Pilling

Illustrated by
JOLYNE KNOX

HEINEMANN · LONDON

For landladies everywhere

William Heinemann Ltd
A division of Reed International Books Ltd
Michelin House
81 Fulham Road
London SW3 6RB

LONDON · MELBOURNE · AUCKLAND

First published 1988
Reprinted 1989 and 1992
Text © 1988 Ann Pilling
Illustrations © 1988 Jolyne Knox
ISBN 0 434 93046 6

Printed in Italy by Olivotto

A school pack of BANANA BOOKS 25-30 is
available from Heinemann Educational Books
ISBN 0 435 00104 3

One big snag

NEIL AND TERRY NUTTER were
twins. They had cheeky red faces and
messy hair and they looked just the
same except for three big freckles on
Terry's bottom. Nobody saw those
except his mum, when he had a bath.
This didn't happen very often because
the Twins thought washing was boring.

Terry and Neil had a greedy fat cat
called Lil. When she was a kitten
they'd called her Lily White, but she
was a dirty grey colour now. She
thought washing was boring too. Her
best friend was Smartie, the black cat
from over the fence.

They all lived at the top of a hill in a funny-shaped house. It was thin at the front and wide at the back and it looked like the last slice of cake on a plate. The garden was messy, like The Twins, because Dad didn't have time to cut the grass. He was away too much, on long trips driving his lorry. So the boys used the garden for jungle warfare.

The slice-of-cake house was bigger than it looked. If you went out at the back and turned left you came to some little steps. At the bottom was a yellow door and behind it there was a whole flat; it went right under The Nutters' kitchen-diner.

This flat was going to be Grandma Nutter's new home. She loved her country cottage but in winter she got snowed up. And it was miles to the shops. Now she was getting old she wanted

to live with Terry and Neil, near town.

But there was one big snag. The flat was already lived in by a grumpy old man called Albert Spencer. He was very tall and very thin and, when he sat in a chair, he had to fold himself up like a penknife. The Twins called him 'Mr Spencer' when Mum was around; when she wasn't they called him 'The Beast'.

The main reason was his long straggly moustache. It was white with brown edges where it had dipped into his tea. Another reason was his bad temper. Albert Spencer never stopped complaining.

Sometimes he complained about Mum's cooking smells. He hated curry and he detested fish. Other times he complained about mice. He said they nibbled at his toes when he lay in bed.

'If you're frightened of mice, Mr Spencer,' Mum said one day, 'why don't you borrow Lil? She could catch them for you.'

But The Beast shook his straggly moustache and glowered. 'Certainly not!' he said snappily. 'I hate cats, especially cats that don't wash themselves.'

He wasn't just bad-tempered, he had funny habits too, like sitting in his deck-chair in the garden, after dark. He also listened to peculiar tapes on his cassette player, whales calling to each other in the middle of the sea, and tigers having fights, and the love song of the Lesser Spotted Nut Popper.

'Why can't he turn it down?' The Twins wanted to know. 'You don't let us play our music that loud.'

'He's a nature lover,' Mum explained.

'He doesn't love mice,' Neil said.

'Or cats,' added Terry.

'Don't argue,' Mum told them. She didn't like quarrels.

But there was a quarrel all the same when The Beast pushed an envelope marked 'Very Important Letter' through the door.

'Dear Mrs Nutter,' it said, 'Although my new flat is ready, I have decided to stay on in your basement. I am working on a special project and cannot be disturbed. Please tell The Twins to stop playing hockey on your kitchen floor. It interrupts my afternoon nap.

Yours truly, Albert Spencer.'

Mum's ears turned pink. 'What's this about hockey?' she said.

'It's not hockey, it's roller skating,' Neil explained.

'What about Gran?' Terry wanted to know. 'He must move out, he *promised*. He's got that new flat in Bank Park to go to anyway.'

'Let's just throw him out,' Neil said, rolling up his sleeves.

'You can't do *that*,' Mum said in alarm. 'Roll down those sleeves this minute. I must talk to your Dad about this, when he gets back from his trip. Meanwhile, I'd better ring Miss Orchard.'

Terry and Neil pulled horrible faces at each other. Miss Orchard was a special lady from the Town Hall who gave people advice and she came to see The Beast quite often. She didn't trust The Twins, with their cheeky red faces, and they didn't trust her. She was bound to stick up for Albert Spencer.

As soon as Mum phoned, she came straight round. She wore a big green hat and carried an enormous handbag. First she went to the downstairs kitchen to talk to The Beast, then she came to the upstairs kitchen and talked to the Nutters. 'I'm very sorry,' she said, 'but he's changed his mind.'

'He *can't*,' Neil told her, 'our Gran's coming. Her cottage gets snowed up in winter and it's three miles from the shops.'

'And he's got his new flat to live in,'

Terry added. 'It's not fair, he *promised* to go.'

'Well, he's working on a special project, that's why he's staying.'

'What sort of project?'

'I don't know, I'm sure. He said it was a secret.'

'Gran was going to let us play in that flat,' Neil said miserably. 'We were getting a dart board and everything.'

Miss Orchard looked suspicious. 'A dart board? For your *grandmother*?'

'Yes, she's good at darts.'

''Well I'm afraid she'll have to stay in the country for a bit, until the special project's finished. Good afternoon,' and Miss Orchard trotted off down the hill, swinging her huge handbag.

'It's no good,' Terry said as they got into bed that night. 'Miss Orchard's on his side and Mum doesn't like quarrels. I wish Dad would come back.'

'We're not waiting for Dad,' Neil told him, snuggling down. 'Perhaps we can't throw him out, but there are other things we can do.' And he fell asleep thinking about them.

Through the Letter-box

NEXT DAY WAS Saturday and they went to see a boy called Brian Ball. He was the cleverest person in their class and a scientific genius. He found things on rubbish tips, took them home and got them working. Then he sold them to people. In a few years time Brian Ball was going to be a millionaire.

Mending and selling things was only

one of his hobbies. Another was pets.
He'd got three goldfish, seven and a
half stick insects and hundreds of white
mice. He'd also got two budgies called
Cagney and Lacey.

Brian Ball had a clever egg-shaped
face and floppy black hair. When he
saw the Twins coming up the path he
just peeped round the door at them
through his little round glasses. But
when he heard what they wanted he let
them in and they followed him upstairs
into his bedroom.

It was chock-full of rubbish with
wires, plugs and screws all over the

floor. The Twins counted three broken hoovers and five battered alarm clocks. For his collection they gave him a pop-up toaster that wouldn't pop and a radio that hissed like a boa-constrictor. In return he gave them a cardboard box that squeaked.

'I want them all back,' he shouted as they carried it down the path, 'I'm only lending them to you. O.K.?'

'O.K.,' The Twins shouted back, as they ran down the road.

On Saturday afternoons The Beast watched sport on telly. Neil and Terry hung about near the dustbin but he heard them and came into his kitchen.

'What do you want?' he yelled, poking his long thin nose through the letter-box, 'and what's that disgusting smell?'

'We don't want anything,' Neil said

'and the smell's only sausages.'

'No, we're just playing.'

'By the dustbin?' The Beast said sourly. 'Go away, you're interrupting my programme.' And the letter-box flapped shut, just missing his nose.

The Twins waited a few minutes, then quietly lifted the flap again and listened hard. The Beast was obviously glued to his T.V. set. They could hear him cheering madly as somebody scored a goal. Terry gave the thumbs-up signal and Neil took the lid off Brian's cardboard box. One by one the wriggly squeaky mice slithered through the slit in the door and plopped down

into the kitchen.

'What if we've killed them?' Terry said nervously. 'That was quite a drop for a mouse.' But when they looked, they could see all six of them racing round the floor. The biggest was trying to creep through the gap under his sitting-room door.

They crept off down the path to the garden shed and sat there, waiting for something to happen.

Five o'clock came. (End of the sports programme.)

Then half past five. (End of the news.)

But there was no sign of The Beast.

What had happened? He was scared stiff of mice. Why didn't he come tearing through his yellow door with a suitcase in each hand?

When the door finally opened, all they saw was a big black shoe.

'Clear off!' yelled The Beast, and slammed it shut again. There sat Lil on the basement steps, looking very pleased with herself.

Terry's mouth dropped open. So did Neil's. Lil's fat furry stomach bulged like a bag full of shopping and she was washing herself for the first time in history.

'It's not worked,' Neil said, in a crushed sort of voice. 'The greedy pig. She must have eaten the lot.'

'What are we going to tell Brian Ball?' asked Terry.

Spies in the Garden

THE SCIENTIFIC GENIUS was not pleased. Lil had gobbled up his white mice and the pop-up toaster still wasn't popping. All he could get on the radio was a spluttery noise like someone being sick. 'You should have made sure Lil wasn't down there,' he said angrily. 'Those mice were worth money. And that stuff you gave me'll never work in a million years. You're just cheats!'

'We're *not*,' Neil told him. 'It's our Gran, we're doing it for our *Gran*,' and they told him about The Beast refusing to go to his fabulous new flat, and about the cottage getting snowed up, and about the special project.

'Special project? What kind of special project?' Brian Ball's little round eyes were gleaming like two snooker balls.

One day he was going to be a great scientist and put stick insects on the moon. 'Perhaps I could help him with it?' he said hopefully.

'Not in Gran's flat,' Neil told him, 'but if you helped us to get rid of him you'd find out what it was, wouldn't you?'

'Go on, Brian,' wheedled Terry. 'You've got brains.'

The genius's face was turning from red to pink again. He liked hearing how clever he was. 'I'll come and see what's happening,' he said pompously, pulling on his anorak. 'Can't promise to do the trick though.'

When they reached home The Beast's front door was shut but he was playing his Lesser Spotted Nut Popper tape very loudly. From his pocket Brian took a folding telescope. 'High-powered

lens,' he whispered, 'brilliant for this job,' and he stuck it through the letter-box.

'What can you see?' Neil muttered.

'Posters. He's got posters stuck all over the kitchen wall. It's dark in there though, I can't read them properly. It says . . . 'Save the—'

'Whale?' suggested Terry.

'Nut Popper?' Neil said, 'he loves those.'

'No. Save the . . . Save the . . . *Hedge*. And there's another one. Fast Roads . . . Kill the Hedge.'

'Save the hedge? Why on earth does he want to save the *hedge*?' Terry

whispered impatiently, prodding Brian
Ball in the bottom.

The scientific genius folded up his
telescope and looked at The Nutters
smugly. 'Ever read the papers?' he said,
'ever watch the news? He's a nature
lover isn't he? Well, hedges are always
buzzing with wildlife. Every time they
cut one down, to build houses or make
a road, things get killed. Hedges are
important,' he told them grandly, 'in
fact they're *historic*. "Fast Roads Kill
the Hedge" – he's obviously raising
money for a special hedge society.'

'Well, why can't he do it in Bank
Park Flats?' Neil said, 'I want to throw

him out, that's what I want.'

'You can't. It's breaking the law.'

'But there must be other things we can do. Don't suppose you've got any ideas, you being a genius and everything?' Neil added slyly.

'I'll sleep on it,' Brian Ball said, swelling with importance. He didn't much care about the Nutters' gran but he cared very much about schemes for making money, and who could say what Albert Spencer was up to, behind that yellow door?

Down the Garden Path

LATE ON SUNDAY night, Terry and Neil were looking through their bedroom window when they saw The

Beast in the garden, creeping through the long grass with a torch.

They slid down the stairs, through the kitchen and out of the back door, but he was already back in his flat, boiling something up on his stove. A ghastly smell was floating out over the garden.

'What a cheek!' Neil whispered. 'He complains about Mum's cooking, then he goes and makes a smell like that.'

'Shut up,' Terry hissed, pulling him down behind the dustbin. 'He's coming out again.'

This time The Beast was carrying a steaming saucepan and a big wooden spoon. They watched him dollop something here and there, in the long grass, then lope back to the flat on his long spindly legs. When he came past they held their noses; the smell from

the pan was like bad eggs, rotten fish
and mouldy rice pudding, rolled into one.

As soon as the yellow door was shut
they explored the garden with Dad's
flashlight. 'Look at this,' Neil said,
'little saucers of milk, all along the
path. And look, a little dish of meat.'

'Ugh, it *stinks*,' Terry whispered.
'What on earth's he playing at?'

But before Neil could answer, the
yellow door had opened yet again and
The Beast came out carrying a stripy
red deckchair. The Twins got back
inside with only seconds to spare.

'What's he doing now?' They'd slid

their bedroom window open and Terry
was leaning right out with Neil holding
on to his feet.

'Sitting in his deckchair and shining
his torch along the path. He's crackers.'

'Perhaps those saucers are cat-traps,'
Neil said. 'The milk's just to lure them
into the garden, but whatever he's
cooked up with the meat kills them off.
He hates Lil and he hates Smartie too.
'He's probably a fur trapper.'

'That's crazy,' Terry told him. 'An old man like that? It can't be true.'

But he was wrong. Next day Lil didn't turn up for breakfast and Smartie didn't come sniffing round either. They were both still missing at dinner time too, Neil ran home from school to check.

The Fur Trapper

AFTER LESSONS THE TWINS cornered Brian Ball in the bikeshed. 'We've found out about the secret project,' they told him, 'and he's a cat trapper. He's raising money for his Hedge Society by skinning cats.' And they explained about the saucers and about The Beast sitting in his deckchair at midnight. 'You could make a nice hat out of cat fur,' Neil said sadly, '*and* gloves. I bet that's what he's doing.'

But Brian Ball looked doubtful. 'You need proof,' he said. 'Have you got any? Taken any photos? Found any fur?'

'Not yet,' Neil admitted, 'but those saucers have disappeared. So have the cats.'

'And he's stuck paper all over his windows,' Terry added 'so whatever he's doing must be pretty disgusting.'

Brian Ball consulted his flashy digital watch with its built-in calculator. 'I can be at your house in an hour,' he said bossily. 'I'll just pop home for my telescope and my camera. Meanwhile,

I'd try and get him out of his flat for a bit, so we can have a look round. If you're right about this cat story you'll need cast-iron evidence. Use your brains, if you've got any,' and he pedalled off. He was still annoyed about Lil eating his mice.

Terry and Neil went straight home. Fortunately, Mum was out; unfortunately, The Beast was in. They could hear his Nut Popper tape loud and clear and he was singing to himself. 'He sounds happy,' Neil said. 'Perhaps he's trapped a few more cats.'

Stealthily they inspected the garden path. There were no more saucers of smelly chopped-up meat but near the basement steps they found a big dish of strawberry jam with flies buzzing round it.

Neil wrinkled up his nose. *'Jam,'* he said 'it's definitely *jam.'*

'But cats don't like jam,' Terry pointed out, 'not even Lil,' and he bent down to pick it up.

'Don't touch it,' Neil warned, 'Brian'll want a photo of that, and a sample for testing.' So they left the jam where it was and went into the house.

The next thing was to get The Beast out of the flat.

'Noise,' Neil said decisively, strapping on his new roller skates, 'let's see what a bit of noise can do,' and he started zooming up and down the kitchen floor. But it was no good, all The Beast did was to turn up his Nut Popper tape extra loud. The sound was deafening.

'O.K., let's flood him out,' Neil said through gritted teeth. Brian Ball was due any minute and they were making no progress at all. 'Do you think we should?' Terry whimpered nervously, watching him uncoil the rubber tubing Mum used for her washing machine.

'Yes I *do*,' Neil replied fiercely, fixing one end to the cold water tap. 'Think of those poor cats. Think of *Gran*. Anything's worth a try.' And he pushed the other end through the window then ran out and shoved it through The Beast's letter-box. Then he turned the water on.

Five minutes later he turned it off again. Gallons of water must have swooshed down that tube but Albert Spencer wasn't reacting. 'Perhaps he's in his sitting room,' Terry said, secretly relieved, 'or having a little snooze.'

'Or making a pair of black and white fur gloves,' Neil added darkly, 'out of Smartie and Lil.'

'I know,' he said, suddenly jumping up, why don't we stink him out? He's always going on about bad smells,' and he ran upstairs to look in the 'One Hundred Jokes and Tricks' box they'd been given for Christmas.

He was soon down again, looking triumphant. 'We've got three left,' he said and he lobbed the stink bombs through the open window. Terry felt sick inside when he heard them land on the basement steps. The Beast had a horrible temper and Mum was miles away, at Gran's. What if he flipped his lid and went for them with a sharp knife? He'd be sure to have one if he was skinning cats.

The smell drifting up from the garden made him feel sicker still. It was like a hundred bad eggs rotting in a hundred sewers. 'Shut the window,' he told Neil, covering up his nose with a wet dish-cloth.

'What on earth's that smell?' said a sharp little voice behind them. 'Nobody answered the front door so I came round the back. Having trouble with your drains are you?' and Brian Ball unloaded his camera and his telescope onto the kitchen table.

'It isn't the drains,' Neil told him, 'it's some stink bombs left over from Christmas. We're trying to stink him out of the flat but we're not having much luck.'

'Oh but you are!' a loud angry voice informed him. The Beast was in the doorway, his face red with rage and his eyes popping. His trousers were pulled up round his hairy ankles and his knobbly bare feet had made wet splodges on the kitchen floor.

'I've had enough of this,' he yelled, waggling his brown and white moustache. 'First you try to deafen me, then you try to drown me. Now you're trying to gas me with horrible smells. Why can't you leave me alone? All I want is peace and quiet, to finish my special project.'

'And we all know what that is, don't we?' Neil yelled back. The Beast sounded so furious the other two had retreated into a corner, but Neil wasn't scared. He kept thinking about Gran and the disappearing cats. 'You should be in prison, you should,' he told him. 'Trapping people's pets to raise money for your silly society. We know just what you're doing and I'm telling Mum about it. She'll ring Miss Orchard.'

The Beast opened and shut his mouth like a hungry goldfish. 'I haven't the least idea what you're talking about,' he said, and his voice had gone very quiet. 'But don't bother ringing Miss Orchard, I rang her myself, to complain about *you*. She's on her way round.'

It was true. Five minutes later she stood on the front door step swinging her handbag and looking very worried. Five minutes after that Mum came back from the country; Gran had come with her. 'It's much too damp in that cottage,' she told The Twins, 'so she's staying in the spare bedroom till the flat's empty. Oh, hello Miss Orchard, nice to see you.' (Terry and Neil pulled faces). 'No more trouble I hope?'

'I'm afraid there is,' Miss Orchard said wearily. 'Now I know Mr Spencer has his funny little ways but your boys have upset him very much indeed, making horrible smells and pouring water through his letter-box. They seem to think he's up to no good, down in your basement flat.'

'He's not, he's a *killer*,' Neil told her, 'and when you find out what he's been doing in there you'll be very surprised indeed.'

Prickles

MISS ORCHARD WENT straight down to the yellow door and everybody else went with her. After half an hour's conversation through the letter-box, The Beast flung the door open and they all trooped in. And they certainly *were* surprised.

The first thing Neil spotted was a black and white fur jacket hanging over a chair. 'There you are Brian,' he said, 'got your camera? This is all that's left of Smartie and Lil.'

'What are you talking about?' said The Beast, picking up the coat. 'I bought this for 50p at the church jumble sale. It was a real bargain. When I've cleaned it up I shall sell it in town, at the Nearly New Shop. The money's for my special project. As for your cats, they'd have starved to death by now if it wasn't for me. They were trapped in Number Five's garage, yowling their heads off. I let them out.'

Neil was still suspicious. 'What about those saucers of milk?' he demanded. 'What about that horrible stuff you boiled up in a pan? What about that saucer of jam you trapped flies with?' But Brian Ball was digging him in the ribs. 'We've made an awful mistake,' he whispered, 'look at the posters. I couldn't see them properly through the letter-box. He's not saving hedges at all.'

Neil and Terry looked. 'Save The Hedgehog' said the blue poster over the cooker, and 'Fast Roads Kill the Hedgehog' said the red one over the sink.

Save The Hedgehog. They'd thought The Beast was skinning cats and selling the fur for money, and all the time it was just a nature project. The Twins had done one themselves in Science. Hedgehogs liked milk and meat, and they adored flies. If only they'd known he'd been trying to save hedgehogs they'd have helped him. They both stared at the wet kitchen floor feeling absolute twits.

Gran was looking round The Beast's kitchen with great interest. This flat was going to be her home one day, after all. 'I'm a nature lover too,' she told him, 'and I've got a hedgehog in my garden. Freddie I call him, I feed him every evening.'

'Well in that case perhaps you'd like to see this.' The Beast opened a large cardboard box and they all took a peep.

Inside were four baby hedgehogs, all fast asleep and making tiny snuffly noises. Neil put his hand out and touched the pinky-brown prickles. They felt warm and soft, not sharp at all.

'Lovely aren't they?' The Beast whispered to Gran in a gooey voice. 'Their poor mother got squashed by a car. Hedgehogs are always getting run over, they need protecting. That's why I'm raising money for this special hedgehog society.'

'I'll join,' Gran said at once, 'and I'll come to the jumble sales with you, too. We might spot another fur-coat . . .'

The two of them were soon chatting away like long-lost friends. Mum and

Miss Orchard went back to the upstairs kitchen with The Twins and Brian Ball. 'If only he'd told us what he was *doing*,' Neil said sheepishly. 'Why did he have to keep it such a big secret?'

'Perhaps he thought you'd laugh at him,' Miss Orchard suggested. 'He's a shy old man.'

'He's getting on well with your grandmother, anyhow. Perhaps she'll make him move into his new flat.'

'She won't,' Terry said gloomily. 'I heard her say he could stay here as long as he wanted. I reckon we're stuck with him and his hedgehogs for ever.'

But they weren't. The Beast moved

out just a week later. Brian Ball said it was because they were making a nature reserve out of the waste ground behind Bank Park Flats. 'That'll mean more hedgehogs,' he explained. 'He can sit and watch them all day and all night if he wants.'

Mum thought it was because he had a crush on Gran. 'They're great friends,' she told Terry and Neil, 'and she's helping him with his hedgehog society now.'

'We know,' The Twins said glumly. (Gran and The Beast got on so well they'd started having nightmares about them getting married.)

'Can't understand what you see in Mr Spencer,' Neil told her one afternoon. They were having a darts match down in her sitting room. 'He was always yelling at us and he never stopped complaining.'

'Oh he's all right when you get to know him,' Gran said. 'He's like those baby hedgehogs really.'

'What do you mean?'

'Well, they look so fierce and spiky but they're ever so soft underneath. People aren't always what they seem you know. Now it's my turn, stand back please.'

And she hit the bull's-eye.